The Lion Who Wouldn't Brush His Teeth

is a gift presented for

Children's Dental Health Education by:

Family Dentists
and
Dr. Judith M. Stitt
Specialist in Orthodontics

A SMILE IS FOREVER

Copyright © 1981 by DENTAL PUBLICATIONS, INC.
P.O. Box 582, Pittsboro, N.C. 27312
All rights reserved, including the right of reproduction
in whole, in part or in any form.

This edition produced exclusively for
  DENTAL MARKETING CONCEPTS
  Post Office Box 667848
  Charlotte, N. C. 28266-7848

Telephone: (704) 865-0199

The lion who wouldn't brush his teeth

Story and pictures
by Mike Peele

Once there was a lion who was king of the jungle.

"That was a nice snack," said the lion as he finished his mid-morning meal of two Jungle burgers and a banana shake.

But the lion never brushed his teeth. "I'm too busy being king of the jungle to bother with that," the lion said as he hurried off.

The lion's breath was so bad from not brushing his teeth that when he roared . . .

the birds dropped from the sky.

The monkeys fell from the trees.

The king thought these animals were passing out because they were AFRAID of him. "Really scared them that time," chuckled the lion as he strolled off.

The animals of the jungle got together to try to decide what to do about the king's breath. "Someone must tell him!" exclaimed the elephant.

All the animals excitedly agreed.

"Now," asked the elephant, "who is going to volunteer?" All the animals became very quiet after that.

"Ahh! A Volunteer!"
cried the elephant.

Before he knew what had happened, Little Monkey was sent out to break the bad news to the king! "You tell him, Little Monkey," cried all the animals.

"Well, what is it?!!" demanded the king. Little Monkey almost fainted but managed to tell the king why he was there.

The king had no idea that his breath was bad. "I'm so embarrassed," he muttered.

"Don't worry," said Little Monkey. "Tomorrow I have an appointment with Dr. Crock, the orthodontist, and my little brother is having his first orthodontic checkup. You can come with us."

"Little Baby Monkey is seven years old now so I've brought him for his first orthodontic examination," announced Little Monkey-- "and the King needs to see Dr. Hippo."

The Orthodontist checked Little Baby Monkey's teeth. "In a few years I'll need to straighten your teeth just like I'm doing on your big brother," said Dr. Crock.

Little Baby Monkey watched as Dr. Crock adjusted Little Monkey's braces. "I can't wait to get my teeth straightened too," he said.

Then it was time for the King to see Dr. Hippo, The Jungle Dentist. "Have a seat," he said, "and I'll check your teeth."

The dentist checked the king's teeth with a little mirror and a pick used for finding cavities.

"Looks like you have chipped off a small piece of this tooth," said Dr. Hippo.

I'll just smooth it up a little with my drill," said Dr. Hippo.

"Don't worry," said Little Monkey. "There's nothing to it."

The dentist cleaned the lion's teeth. Then he shined them with a special polisher.
"That tickles," said the king.

"Wow," said the king when he saw how shiny his teeth were.

"They look great, and they feel great, too!"

"I'll always be sure to brush every day," said the king.

"And don't forget to floss too," said Little Monkey.

The king was very grateful to Little Monkey for telling him about his breath.

"Come on pal, let's go play some soccer," said the king.

THE END

Important Facts About Dental Care

Taking Care of Your Child's Teeth

The American Dental Association has recommended that the proper age for a child's first visit to a family dentist is 2 years. By that time, most of the child's primary teeth are visible and can be easily checked and cleaned. Upon the first visit to the dentist, instructions will be given to both the child and parents about: proper brushing and flossing; advice on proper diet and nutrition; the use of fluorides and other preventive measures necessary to stop tooth decay. By following these instructions, a child can have cavity-free teeth and better all around health. It is important to know that dental care in the pre-school years—and until the age of 6—is the parents' responsibility rather than the child's.

Preventive Dentistry - A Checklist For Your Child

Using the following checklist can help your child develop proper oral hygiene habits throughout his or her life.

Diet & Nutrition - Eating the right foods helps build strong teeth. A good diet should provide a balance of the four food groups: milk and dairy products, meat and fish, bread and cereals, and fruit and vegetables. These foods have all the vitamins and minerals necessary for general body growth and health as well as good sound dental development. It is important to establish good diet and eating habits throughout the pre-school years of your children. Ask your dentist or pediatrician for a balanced diet plan.

Good Brushing Habits - Your child should brush after every meal or snack when possible. For orthodontic patients this is an absolute necessity. How well children clean their teeth depends on two factors: the teaching and supervision furnished by the parent, and the example set by the parent.

Flossing - It is important to teach a child to floss their teeth at least once a day - usually before brushing or after the evening meal. Dental floss helps clean between and on the sides of your child's teeth where the toothbrush cannot reach.

Toothpaste - Toothpaste is used to help remove plaque and stains, polish the teeth and leave the mouth with a pleasant taste and refreshing feeling. A fluoride toothpaste is recognized by the American Dental Association as being effective in reducing tooth decay in children and adults. Studies show that by using a fluoride toothpaste, tooth decay can be reduced by 25% or more.

Fluorides - The most common sources of natural fluoride are our saliva, the foods we eat, and the water we drink. Another common source of fluoride can be found in some toothpastes and mouth rinses. Fluorides are a safe method to battle against and prevent dental decay in children and adults.

Toothbrush - A toothbrush that works the best for children is one that has a small head, a straight handle and soft bristles that won't scratch the gums. Another good use of the tooth brush is for brushing the top surface of the tongue.

Disclosing Tablets - These are chewable tablets that leave bright red spots on your child's teeth after brushing. They show missed plaque on your child's teeth and should be rebrushed until the stains disappear. Special attention should be paid to those areas in everyday brushing.

Regular Check-Ups - It is important to take your child to the dentist on a regular basis - usually every six months. Regular check-ups help the dentist check for decay and proper positioning of your child's teeth. If decay or other dental problems have occured, it will be detected in the early stages when it is easier and less costly to treat.

Dental Words To Know

Canine	Pointed teeth used for tearing food.
Cavity	A hole in the tooth caused by decay or "sugar bugs".
Decay	Caused by bacteria (germs) which eat away the tooth.
Dental Floss	Thin thread used to clean between the teeth.
Dentist	A person who takes care of your teeth.
Disclosing Tablets	Chewable tablets that leave bright red spots on teeth where the toothbrush did not clean.
Enamel	The white outside covering of a tooth.
Filling	A material used by the dentist to replace decay in the tooth.
Fluoride	A natural element found in drinking water and many foods. Also, found in toothpaste and mouthrinses - helps prevent decay.
Hygienist	A person who checks, cleans and may seal teeth.
Incisor	Front flat teeth used for biting food.
Molar	A large tooth in the back of the mouth used for grinding food.
Plaque	A sticky film which forms on teeth.
Sealant	A coat of plastic material applied to the grooves of a tooth to prevent decay.
"Sugar Bugs"	Bacteria (germs) which feed on sugar in your mouth.
Tartar	A hard substance that forms on teeth if plaque is not removed.
X-Rays	Pictures taken of your teeth by a special camera.

Orthodontics

The American Association of Orthodontists has recommended that the proper age for a child's first visit to an orthodontist is age 7. Early examination by an orthodontist can detect any present or future conditions that may require orthodontic treatment. Then orthodontic treatment is started at the right time, it will cost less money, take less time and treatment will be more successful. During your child's first visit, the orthodontist will examine the teeth and all related structures—the lips, tongue and facial muscles.

Early Warning Signs That Orthodontic Treatment Is Needed

There are two general causes of orthodontic problems: **acquired** and **inherited.**

Inherited causes — One child in three inherits orthodontic problems such as missing, crowded, extra or too large teeth. Also deformities in the jaw and face are inherited causes.

Acquired causes — These are caused by thumb-sucking, lip biting, abnormal swallowing and dental disease. Not only do these problems affect the teeth but the facial appearance as well.

By and large, most people seek orthodontic treatment because their teeth do not look good. Appearance is the main reason an individual seeks orthodontic treatment. We live in a world where a bright smile and straight, even teeth contribute to an individual's personality and self-confidence. The orthodontist's primary goal is to improve oral health which in turn improves one's looks and emotional well being. Remember it is never too early for a visual examination of a child if a parent is suspicious of an orthodontic problem.

Orthodontic Words To Know

Active Retainer	Similar to a retainer but used for children with minor crooked teeth.
Appliance	A removable or fixed orthodontic piece.
Bands	Metal strips that fit around the tooth.
Braces	A corrective appliance used to straighten teeth.
Bracket	An orthodontic brace that is glued to the tooth.
Headgear	A wire piece and neck pad used on upper teeth for children with buck teeth.
Malocclusion	Crooked, crowded or protruding teeth.
Orthodontic Model	A plaster model of your teeth used for studying purposes by the orthodontist.
Orthodontics	Science of straightening teeth.
Orthodontist	A specialist who straightens teeth and who has completed two additional years of dental school.
Retainer	Used after braces to hold teeth in their new position enabling them to become stronger.
Rubber Bands	Used to correct the position of teeth or jaws. They are hooked to the braces.
Separators	Small rubber strips placed between teeth to widen them when bands are to be fitted on teeth.
Space Maintainer	A metal piece used for maintaining space between teeth which was caused by premature loss of a tooth.